HENRY

JAMES

D0717536

PERCY

MEET ALL THESE FRIENDS IN BUZZ BOOKS:

Thomas the Tank Engine
The Animals of Farthing Wood
Biker Mice from Mars
Winnie-the-Pooh
Fireman Sam
Rupert
Babar

First published in Great Britain 1993 by Buzz Books,
an imprint of Reed Children's Books
Michelin House, 81 Fulham Road, London SW3 6RB
and Auckland, Melbourne, Singapore and Toronto
Reprinted 1993, 1994 (twice), 1995

Copyright © William Heinemann Limited 1993
All publishing rights: William Heinemann Ltd
All television and merchandising rights
licensed by William Heinemann Limited to
Britt Allcroft (Thomas) Limited, exclusively, worldwide

Photographs © Britt Allcroft (Thomas) Ltd 1992
Photographs by David Mitton and Terry Permane
for Britt Allcroft's production of
Thomas the Tank Engine and Friends

ISBN 1 85591 290 2

Printed and bound in Italy by Olivotto

TRUST THOMAS

buzz books

Thomas the Tank Engine was feeling bright and cheerful. It was a splendid day.

"Good morning," he whistled to some cows, but the cows didn't reply.

"Never mind," said Thomas. "They're busy with their breakfast."

Next he saw Bertie.

"Hello, Bertie. Care for a race today?"

But all Bertie could say was, "Ouch! That's another hole in the road."

"I'm sorry, Bertie," smiled Thomas.

Thomas was still in good spirits when
Bertie arrived at the next station.

"Bad luck, Bertie," said Thomas. "Now
if you were a steam engine, you would run
on a pair of reliable rails."

"Huh," replied Bertie. "The railway was supposed to deliver tar to mend the road two weeks ago. You can't trust a thing that runs on rails."

"I run on rails. You can trust me, Bertie. I'll see if I can find out what's happened."

Thomas left Bertie and made his way along the branch line towards the big station by the sea.

James was snorting about in the yard.

"It's too bad. Percy goes to work at the harbour and I do his job — here, there and everywhere. Take that!"

"Ooh!" groaned the trucks. "Just you wait. We'll show you."

Gordon laughed. "I'll tell you what, James. If you pretended to be ill *everywhere*, you couldn't shunt trucks *here* or go to the quarry *there*, could you?"

"What a good idea!" agreed James. "Look! Here comes Thomas. I'll start pretending now."

Thomas was sorry to see the engines looking miserable.

"Cheer up. It's a beautiful day."

"Yes," grumbled Gordon, "but not for James."

"What's the matter?"

"He's sick," replied Gordon.

"Yes, he is. I mean, I am," stuttered James. "I don't feel well at all."

"Don't worry," said Thomas kindly. "I'll help out if you're ill."

Gordon and James sniggered quietly to each other.

Some of James's trucks were coupled behind Thomas and he steamed away to the quarry.

The trucks were still cross.

"We couldn't pay James back for bumping us, so we'll play tricks on Thomas instead. One engine is as good as another."

But Thomas didn't hear them. He collected all the stone from the quarry and then set off back to the junction. Danger lay ahead.

"Now for our plan," giggled the trucks. "Go faster, go faster!"

"Slow down," called Thomas's driver and applied the brakes.

Poor Thomas stood dazed and surprised in a muddy pond as a toad eyed him suspiciously.

"Bust my buffers," muttered Thomas. "The day started so well, too."

Duck pulled away the trucks, and Edward helped Thomas back to the junction.

Suddenly Thomas remembered the missing tar. He told Edward all about it.

"That's strange," said Edward. "A truck full of tar has been left at my station. That must be it. Driver will make sure it gets to Bertie now."

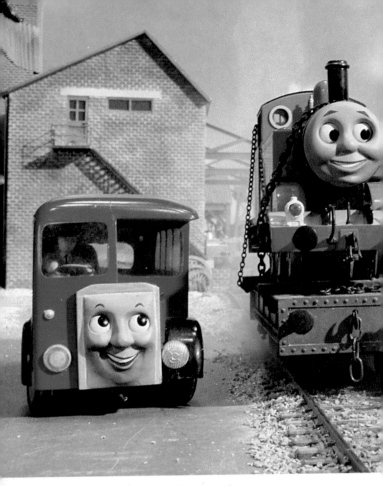

Later, James spoke to Thomas.

"I'm sorry about your accident," he muttered. "And so is Gordon. We didn't mean to get you into trouble."

"No indeed," spluttered Gordon. "A mere misunderstanding, Thomas. All's well that ends well."

Just then Bertie arrived. He looked much more cheerful.

"My road's being mended now."

"Oh, I am glad," replied Thomas.

"Thanks for all you did. Now I know I can trust an engine, especially if his name is Thomas."

Gordon and James puffed silently away to the shed!

But Thomas still had company.

"Well, well," he sighed. "What a day for surprises."

The toad, who was looking forward to a ride home, noisily agreed.

THOMAS

EDWARD

GORDON